W9-BYD-310

TO ALL CHILDREN

A pleasant sound,
A Merry-Go-Round
Of stories old
And stories new,
Gathered here
For all of you.
—M. G.

Watercolor paints and a black pen were used for the full-color art.
The text type is Veljovic Book.

THE STRONGEST ONE OF ALL, based on a Caucasian folktale, was first published in 1977 by Greenwillow Books. WHAT KIND OF BIRD IS THAT?, adapted from a Russian story by V. Suteyev, was first published in 1973 by Crown Publishers, Inc. WHERE DOES THE SUN GO AT NIGHT?, adapted from an Armenian song, was first published in 1981 by Greenwillow Books. THE FOX AND THE HARE, based on a Russian folktale, was first published in 1969 by Crown Publishers, Inc.

Printed in Singapore by Tien Wah Press First Edition 10 9 8 7 6 5 4 3 2 1

Library of Congress Cataloging-in-Publication Data
Ginsburg, Mirra.
Merry-go-round: four stories / by Mirra Ginsburg;
pictures by Jose Aruego and Ariane Dewey.
p. cm.
Summary: A collection of four fables featuring animal characters.
ISBN 0-688-09256-X. ISBN 0-688-09257-8 (lib. bdg.)
1. Fables. [1. Fables. 2. Animals—Fiction.] I. Aruego, Jose, ill.
II. Dewey, Ariane, ill. III. Title. PZ8.2.G5St 1992
[E]—dc20 90-30439 CIP AC

C O N T E N T S

THE STRONGEST ONE OF ALL

A lamb slipped on the ice and cried,
"Ice, ice, you made me fall. Are you strong?
Are you the strongest one of all?"

But the ice answered, “If I were the strongest, would the sun melt me?”

The lamb went to the sun and asked, “Sun, sun, are you the strongest one of all?”
But the sun answered, “If I were the strongest, would the cloud cover me?”

The lamb went to the cloud and asked, "Cloud, cloud, are you the strongest one of all?"

But the cloud answered, "If I were the strongest, would I scatter into rain?"

The lamb went to the rain and asked, "Rain, rain, are you the strongest one of all?"

But the rain answered, "If I were the strongest, would the earth swallow me?"

The lamb went to the earth and asked, "Earth, earth, are you the strongest one of all?"

But the earth answered, "If I were the strongest, would the grass push its roots down through me, push its shoots up through me?"

The lamb went to the grass and asked, "Grass, grass, are you the strongest one of all?"

But the grass answered, "If I were the strongest, would a lamb pluck me, would a lamb eat me?"

And the lamb leaped with joy.
"I may slip, and I may fall,
but I'm the strongest!
I'm the strongest of them all!"

WHAT KIND OF BIRD IS THAT?

Once upon a time there lived a goose. He envied everybody and was always quarreling and hissing, "S-s-s! S-s-s!"

All the other birds and animals and people shook their heads and said, "My, what a very silly goose."

One day the goose saw a swan on the lake. He liked the swan's long neck. "If only I could have a neck like that!" he thought. "Let us trade," he said to the swan. "I'll give you my neck, if you will give me yours."

The swan thought it over and agreed.

The goose walked on with the long swan neck and did not know what to do with it.
He turned it, he stretched it, he rolled it up like a wheel.
But no matter what he did, he was not comfortable.

"You are neither goose nor swan! Ha-ha-ha!" laughed a pelican.

The goose was insulted and wanted to hiss, but suddenly he noticed the pelican's beak with the large sack under it.

"Ah, if only I could have such a beak," thought the goose. "Let us trade," he said to the pelican. "I'll give you my beak, if you will give me yours."

The pelican laughed and agreed.

"How clever I am," thought the goose. "Now I can get everything I want by trading, and I will become the finest goose in the world."

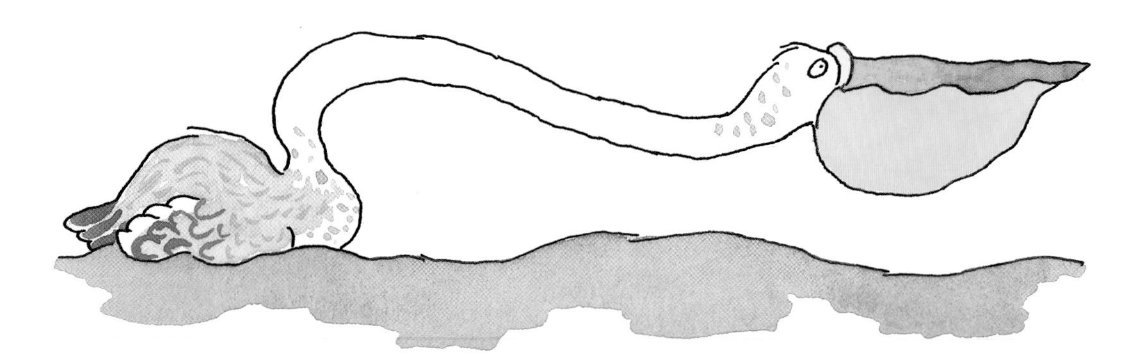

He traded legs with the crane. In exchange for
his short legs with the flat, webbed feet, he got the
crane's long, slender legs.
He traded his large white wings for the crow's
little black wings.

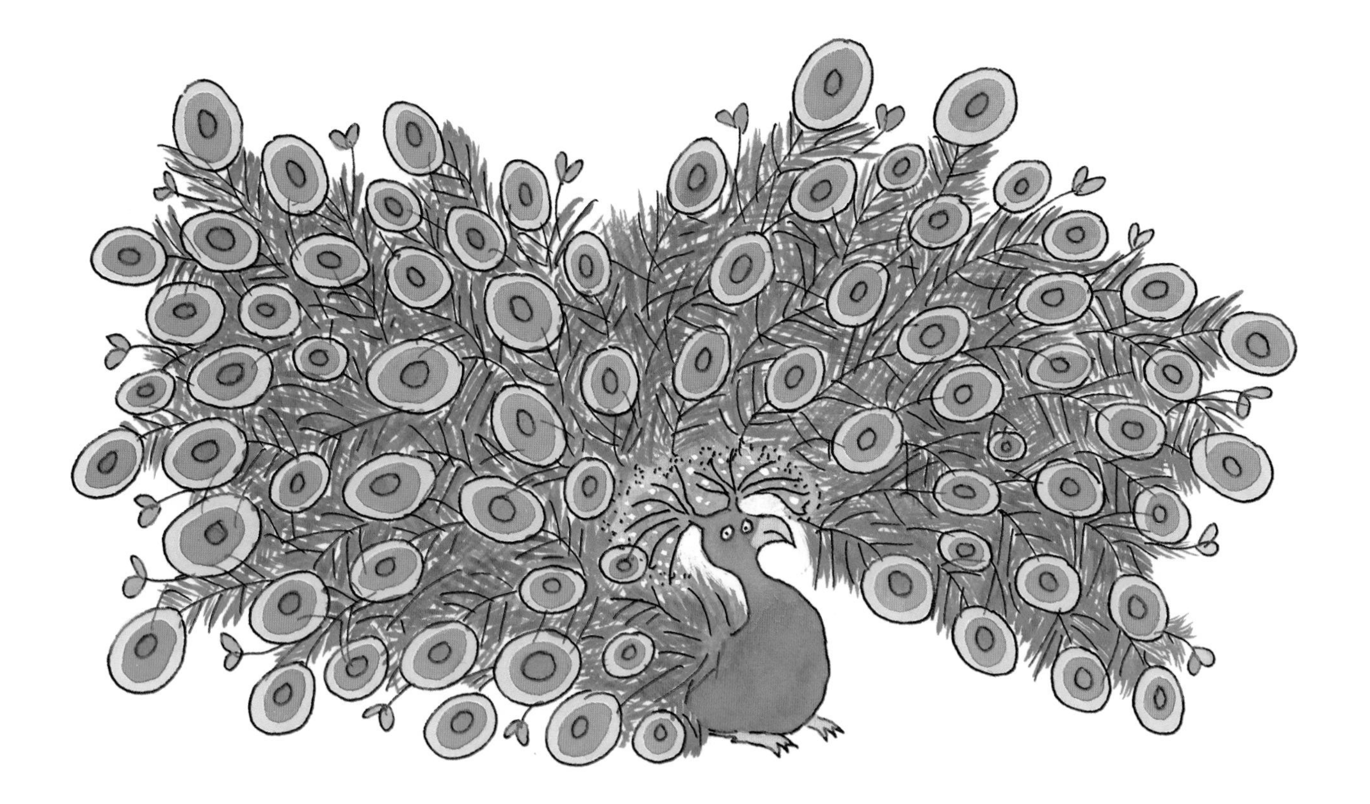

Then he saw a peacock opening and closing his great shimmering tail. It took the goose a long time to convince the peacock to trade it for his own short tail that could only waggle from side to side. But the peacock finally got tired of the goose and traded with him.

When the goose had nothing more to trade, the kindhearted rooster simply gave him his comb, his wattle, and even his loud, ringing "Cock-a-doodle-doo."

Now the goose looked like no other bird in the world. He strode on the crane's long legs, proudly waving the great peacock tail and turning the long swan neck this way and that, until he met a flock of geese.

"Ga-ga-ga! What kind of bird is that?" wondered the geese.

"I am a goose!" cried the goose. He flapped the crow's wings, stretched the swan's neck, and sang out with the pelican's huge beak, "Cock-a-doodle-doo! I am the most beautiful goose on earth!"

"Well, if you are a goose, come with us," said the geese.

They came to a field. All the geese plucked the fresh, sweet grass, but the goose could only clack his enormous beak with its sack. The beak was made for catching fish, and the goose could not pluck a single blade of grass with it.

Then the geese went to the lake to swim, and the goose went with them. They swam merrily, but the goose could only run back and forth along the bank. The crane's long legs were made for wading, not for swimming.

"Ga-ga-ga!" laughed the geese.

"Cock-a-doodle-doo!" answered the goose.

The geese came out of the water.
Suddenly a fox jumped out of the reeds. The geese spread their wings and rose into the air.
Only the goose remained. The crow's little wings could not lift him up.

He started running on the crane's legs, but the peacock's splendid tail got tangled in the reeds. The fox caught him by the swan's long neck. But the geese came flying from all directions, beating the fox with their wings and pecking him with their beaks. The fox let the goose go and ran for dear life.

WHERE DOES THE SUN GO AT NIGHT?

Where does the sun go at night?
To his grandma's house.

Where does he sleep?
In his grandma's bed.
Who is his grandma?
The deep blue sky.

What is he covered with?
A woolly cloud.
Who tucks him in?
His grandpa.

Who is his grandpa?
The wind.

What does he dream about?
The moon and the stars.

Who wakes him up?
The morning.

Who wakes the morning?
The alarm clock.
Who is the clock?

The village cock.

THE FOX AND THE HARE

There were once two neighbors, a fox and a hare.
The fox lived in a house made of ice.
The hare lived in a house made of wood.
All winter the fox teased the hare,

"My house is bright, your house is dark!
My house is bright, your house is dark!"

Spring came, and the sun rose high, and the fox's house melted away. But the hare's house was still as good as new.
The fox had no place to sleep. He came to the hare and begged, "Please let me in for the night."
But the hare said, "No. You laughed at me all winter. I won't let you in."

The fox asked once, and the fox asked twice, and the third time the hare took pity on him. He opened the door, and the fox came in. And as soon as he was in, he took the broom and chased the hare out.

The hare walked down the road, crying bitterly.
Then he met a dog.
"Woof, woof! Why are you crying?"
And the hare said, "How can I help crying?
I had a wood house, and the fox had an ice house.
He asked me to let him in, and he chased me out."
"Don't cry, little hare! I will help you."

They came to the house, and the dog barked,
"Woof, woof! Who is under that roof?
Bow-wow! Get out now!"
But the fox replied from his nice cozy bed,
"I'll come out, I'll jump out!
I will scratch your eyes out!"
The dog got frightened and ran away.

Again the hare walked down the road, crying.
Then he met a bear.

"Why are you crying, little hare?"

"How can I help crying? I had a wood house, and the fox had an ice house. He asked me to let him in, and he chased me out."

"Don't cry. I will help you!"

"No, you won't! The dog could not help me, and neither will you."

"Oh, yes, I will. Just watch me!"

They came to the house, and the bear growled,
"Ho-ho-ho!
You'd better go!"
But the fox replied from his nice cozy bed,
"I'll come out, I'll jump out!
I will scratch your eyes out!"
The bear got frightened and ran away.

The hare walked down the road again, till he met a bull.

"Why are you crying, little hare?"

"How can I help crying? I had a wood house, and the fox had an ice house. He asked me to let him in, and he chased me out."

"Come, I will help you!"

"No, you won't! The dog could not help me, and the bear could not help me, and neither will you."

"Oh, yes, I will. Just watch me!"

They came to the house, and the bull bellowed,

"Moo-whoo!
Out with you!"

But the fox replied from his nice cozy bed,

"I'll come out, I'll jump out!
I will scratch your eyes out!"

The bull got frightened and ran away.

The hare walked down the road again, till he met a rooster.

"Cock-a-doodle-doo! What's the matter with you? Why are you crying?"

"How can I help crying? I had a wood house, and the fox had an ice house. He asked me to let him in, and he chased me out."

"Is that all? Come, I will help you."

"No, you won't! The dog could not help me, and the bear could not help me, and the bull could not help me, and neither will you."

"Oh, yes, I will. Just come and see!"

They came to the house, and the rooster made a great big noise. He stamped his feet, and he flapped his wings, and he pecked at the window.

"I'll crow and I'll shout,
Cock-a-doodle-doo!
If you don't get out,
I'll come after you!"

The fox got frightened and cried, "Just let me put my shoes on!"

The rooster stamped his feet a second time, and he flapped his wings, and he pecked at the window.

"I'll crow and I'll shout,
Cock-a-doodle-doo!
If you don't get out,
I'll come after you!
I have sharp black spurs.
Look out for your furs!"

And the fox begged, "Just let me get dressed!"

The rooster stamped his feet a third time, and he flapped his wings, and he pecked at the window.

"I'll crow and I'll shout,
Cock-a-doodle-doo!
If you don't get out,
I'll come after you!
I have sharp black spurs.
Look out for your furs!
Ko-ko-ko!
Out you go!
Now!"

"I'm going, I'm going," cried the fox.

He ran out of the house and slunk through the grass and into the bushes and across the field and off and away to the far, far woods.

He ran so fast that all you could see was his red tail flashing.